Pasture Bedtime

written & illustrated by
Anne Vernon

Roundtree Press

How does it feel to sit by the moon, eating yogurt and fresh ice cream with a spoon?

How does it feel to
chew grass all day long,
with a moo and a moo-ahhh
as we sing our spring song?

Everyday grazing and everyday smells
fill up our bellies and keep us all well.

Never a worry or care in our lives, greeting the bees as they hum in their hives.

Little calves napping, so snug in their hay,
while mama is busy making milk every day.

Dancing and prancing
in grass all around,
our pasture is perfect,
and nature abounds.

Cookie and Poppy and Lucky, so proud,
have discovered a bull sleeping up in a cloud!

Healthy and happy and rich in sunshine,
our sweet little calves run and tumble in time.

Organically fed
and so naturally so,
they prosper and thrive,
and they sing as they grow.

Mama and Farmer Dan
care for their health.
They dance in the sun and grow
strong with health's wealth.

Cookie, Poppy, and Lucky play down by the pond.
So happy and mucky, mud baths make them yawn.

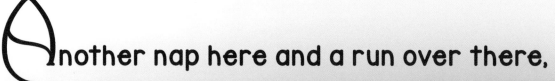

Another nap here and a run over there,

they sleep and they eat and they trot in fresh air!

Chasing the fireflies
at dusk in the field,
they now wish on a star
that the day once concealed.

"Quick Cookie! Run Lucky! Fast Poppy! Come here!"
Clo shouts out with three good-hearted cheers.

It's time for your bedtime,
time to rest and dream, dears.

It's way Pasture Bedtime, my sweet little dears.

It's way Pasture Bedtime, my sweet little dears.

My sweet little marvelous, wonderful dears . . .

About Clo the Cow

Clo the Cow, Sonoma County's legendairy bovine, is the beloved mascot of Clover Sonoma – socialite, advertising genius, and mama to Cookie, Poppy, and Lucky! Grazing the fronts of billboards, milk cartons, and public events throughout the San Francisco North Bay, she is one very busy bovine, whose legacy has been deeply rooted in Northern California's agricultural and dairy communities for over fifty years.

The story of Clo began in 1969, when Clover founder Gene Benedetti and advertising pioneer Lee Levinger came up with the idea of a cartoon cow whose pun-filled billboards would bring a lightheartedness to commuters. At first, the board of directors thought the idea was udder nonsense, but ultimately, they decided to give it a shot! When artist Bill Nellor drew the first Clo billboard, "Support Your Local Cow," which debuted on Highway 101 in Rohnert Park, California, no one had ever seen such a captivating smile (or any smile, for that matter) on a cow. Since that debut, Clo has become a cherished icon of the North Bay, with artwork done by Jim Benefield, and for the last twenty-five years, Anne Vernon (illustrator and author of this book).

To this day, Gene's vision for Clo stands true. In everything she does, whether smiling on a billboard or passing out hugs and high-fives at a public event, Clo is a beacon of light and laughter in her local community. It is in this spirit that the Clover Cares Giveback Program was formed – a commitment to invest at least 5 percent of annual profits to support what's dear to us here at Clover Sonoma: local agriculture, empowering future generations, and supporting the community at large.

For more information about Clover Sonoma, please visit: cloversonoma.com

Gene Benedetti and Clo

Dedicated with love
to Violet, Cedar & Clo

Library of Congress Cataloging-in-Publication Data available.
ISBN: 978-1-949480-06-1

Printed in China.   10 9 8 7 6 5 4 3 2 1

Produced by Clover Sonoma
cloversonoma.com

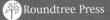 Roundtree Press

Petaluma, California 94952
www.roundtreepress.com